Itsy Bitsy Spider

by Keith Chapman

Illustrated by Jack Tickle

tiger tales

whooosh!

Itsy Bitsy Spider,
playing on a farm.
Spinning silver silk webs,
high up in a barn.

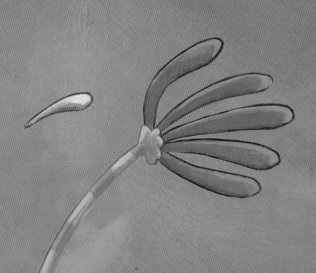

From an open window,
a gust of wind blows WHOOOSH!

Swooooosh!

And Itsy Bitsy Spider
with a SWOOOOOSH
goes, too!

Itsy Bitsy Spider
is flying, there he goes!
He drifts on to a pink pig
and dangles from its nose.

OINKKK! grunts the pig
with Itsy climbing up his snout.
And Itsy Bitsy Spider
is catapulted out!

Oinkkk!

Itsy Bitsy Spider,
he doesn't think it's funny.
He's tangled on a gray goat
and calls out for his mommy.

B-E-H-H-H-H-H! bleats the goat,
who shakes from side to side.
And Itsy Bitsy Spider
begins another ride!

Behhhhh!

Itsy Bitsy Spider,
can you see him now?
He's fluttered on to Buttercup,
the black-and-white young cow.

MOOOO! says Buttercup
and flicks her long, wide ears.
And Itsy Bitsy Spider
spins off and disappears!

MOOOO!

Itsy Bitsy Spider,
gliding through the air.
He hangs on to a duck's bill
and tickles under there.

QUACK! honks the yellow duck,
and gives a great big sneeze.
And Itsy Bitsy Spider
floats off in the breeze!

Quack!

Itsy Bitsy Spider,
what a dizzy day!
He's settled on a brown horse
chewing clumps of hay.

Neig

NEIGHHHH! snorts the horse,
and jumps up really high.
Then Itsy Bitsy Spider
takes off through the sky!

hhhh!

Itsy Bitsy Spider,
clever little thing.
He shoots out lines of web silk
and sticks to rooster's wing.

Cock-a-doodle-doo!

The red, feathered
rooster crows
COCK-A-DOODLE-DOO!
But Itsy Bitsy Spider,
where on earth are you?

Itsy Bitsy Spider,
what's he stuck on now?
A goat, horse, or rooster?
A pig, duck, or cow?

No, he bounces with a

Boinnggg!

Hooray! It's Mommy's web!
Now Itsy Bitsy Spider
is safely home in bed!

tiger tales

an imprint of ME Media, LLC

202 Old Ridgefield Road, Wilton, CT 06897

Published in the United States 2006

Originally published in Great Britain 2005

By Little Tiger Press

An imprint of Magi Publications

Text copyright © 2006 Keith Chapman

Illustrations copyright © 2006 Jack Tickle

CIP data is available

ISBN 1-58925-055-9

Printed in China

All rights reserved

1 3 5 7 9 10 8 6 4 2